Dear Parent:
Your child's love of reading starts here!

Every child learns to read in a different way and at his or her own speed. Some go back and forth between reading levels and read favorite books again and again. Others read through each level in order. You can help your young reader improve and become more confident by encouraging his or her own interests and abilities. From books your child reads with you to the first books he or she reads alone, there are I Can Read Books for every stage of reading:

SHARED READING
Basic language, word repetition, and whimsical illustrations, ideal for sharing with your emergent reader

BEGINNING READING
Short sentences, familiar words, and simple concepts for children eager to read on their own

READING WITH HELP
Engaging stories, longer sentences, and language play for developing readers

READING ALONE
Complex plots, challenging vocabulary, and high-interest topics for the independent reader

I Can Read Books have introduced children to the joy of reading since 1957. Featuring award-winning authors and illustrators and a fabulous cast of beloved characters, I Can Read Books set the standard for beginning readers.

A lifetime of discovery begins with the magical words **"I Can Read!"**

Visit www.icanread.com for information
on enriching your child's reading experience.

Super Wings: Lost Stars
Copyright © 2019 FUNNYFLUX / ALPHA
All rights reserved. Printed in the United States of America.
No part of this book may be used or reproduced in any manner whatsoever without written permission
except in the case of brief quotations embodied in critical articles and reviews. For information address
HarperCollins Children's Books, a division of HarperCollins Publishers,
195 Broadway, New York, NY 10007.
www.icanread.com

ISBN 978-0-06-290722-6

19 20 21 22 23 LSCC 10 9 8 7 6 5 4 3 2 1 ❖ First Edition

LOST STARS

Adapted by Steve Foxe
Based on the episode "Constellation Situation"
by Hugh Duffy & Andrew Sabiston

HARPER
An Imprint of HarperCollinsPublishers

I am Jett.

Sometimes I'm a plane.

Sometimes I'm a robot.

I take boxes across the world.
This box is going to Italy.

"I'm Jett!" I say.

"I'm on time, every time.
This box is for you."

"Thank you," the girl says.
"Now I can look at the stars
all the time!"

"Look," the girl says.

"Stars tell a story."

"Do you see the circle?"

"The circle is part of this story," the girl says.

It's getting dark outside.

"Come on," the girl says.

"I'll show you."

Oh no!

The circle is missing!

I call Astra and her friends.

They are spaceships.

They can find the lost stars!

"Hop in," I say.

we fly up, up, up.

"It's trash!" the girl says.

"Trash is in front of the stars."

"That's why we can't see the circle of stars."

We see a spaceship.

"Nimbus Ned," the ship says.

"Ready to clean!"

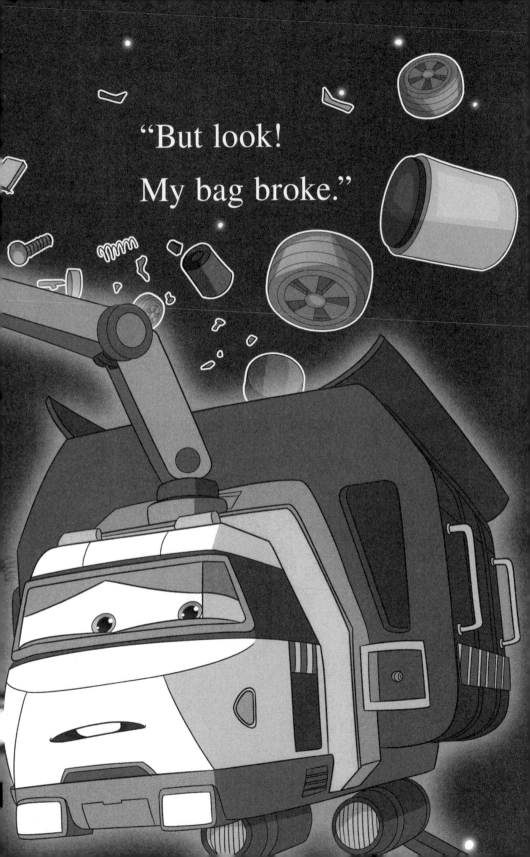

"Don't worry," Astra says.
"We can help!"

Astra and her friends
clean up the junk.

The trash is gone.

We can see the stars again.

"We did it!" the girl says.

The girl smiles.

"We saved the day!" she says.

"No," I say.

"We saved the stars!"

Super Wings saved the stars!